Caterina's Journey

An Italian-American Immigration Story

Author Maryann Pisano

Illustrator Jennise Conley

Illustrations Adapted From Lisa Lucchese

To anyone who ever had a dream...
follow it!

Once upon a time, in Reggio Di Calabria, Italy, lived a little girl named Caterina Tolitano. Caterina loved her home! She loved gazing at the mountains and playing outside under a warm, deep blue sky. Caterina also loved to play with her friends Marianna, Piero, and Rosa.

In the morning, Caterina's mom, Mamma Filomena would bake fresh bread.

She would even help her Papa` Antonio catch dinner straight from the sea!

One day, Papa` Antonio told Caterina that they were going to move to America.

Caterina was sad. She didn't want to leave her town. But Papa` Antonio said, "Caterina, America is the land of opportunity! The streets are paved with gold!"

So, Papa Antonio, Mamma Filomena, Caterina and her brothers Domenico and Giuseppe set sail on a large boat. They traveled across the Atlantic Ocean for 30 days to America.

Caterina didn't like the boat ride. It was dirty and stuffy. She even got a little seasick.

Each day, the family was served a box lunch. One day they were served bananas. Caterina and her family didn't know what a banana was. They didn't have that in Italy. Giuseppe took a bite of the banana-- peel and all!

Finally, Papa` Antonio said, "Caterina, look, it's the Statue of Liberty!"

Caterina and her family landed on Ellis Island and waited in line for three days to enter America.

Caterina did not like America at first. She looked different from other children and did not understand English. Some of the kids even laughed at her.

Mrs. Scott, her sixth grade teacher, was mean to her. "She does not belong here!" she said. "She should go back to her own country!" Mrs. Scott put Caterina in a first grade classroom. Caterina felt silly because all the other kids were much younger than her.

Life was not easy for her family, either. Papa` Antonio came home from work tired and dirty. Domenico and Giuseppe couldn't go to school-- they had to find jobs to help the family.

But, Caterina and her family didn't give up.She worked hard to learn English. Soon, school became easier.

She made friends and loved reading books. She was proud to be American.

Today, Caterina tells her grandchildren about how she came to America as an immigrant.

Caterina's grandchildren are proud to be Italian- American. So is Caterina!

And to this day, Giuseppe still does not eat bananas!

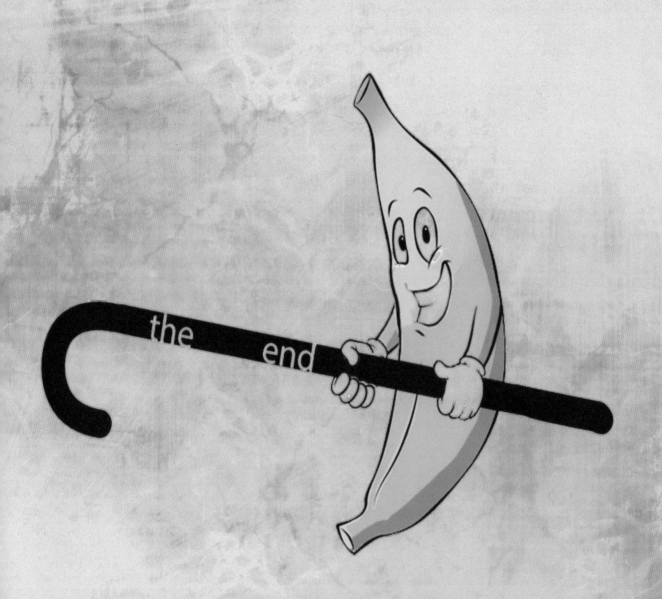

There are so many people I want to thank I don't even know where to start! First of all, thank you to my friends who have stood by my side through the thick and the thin. You know who you are!

Thank you to my una cara amica Mariangela Pezzella for helping me with all the Italian translations. Grazie bella!

Thank you to all my teachers at Rhodes School who have always encouraged me keep writing, writing, writing! Thank you to Mr. Rossi for keeping me interested in journalism and to Dr. Hughes for always contributing to Emme Magazine.

Thank you to Jill Oswald for helping with me the technology portion of this book—you are fabulous!

A BIG thank you to all my aunts, uncles, and cousins for supporting my writing career. Your support means more to me than you'll ever know.

Thank you to my angel in Heaven, my grandfather, Grandpa Pat. You will forever be my hero! Thank you to my Grandma Antoinette for your support. Your story is next! Thank you to my other guardian angels, my Grandma Catherine and Grandpa Joe. Your journeys were the inspiration for this book.

Thank you to my brother Anthony. You are an amazing brother-- I love you!

MOST IMPORTANTLY thank you to my PARENTS! My writing career would not exist without you. Thank you for everything you do for me. Your love makes all things possible!

Lisa—we did it, cugina! You are an amazing artist. I couldn't have done this without you.

Thank you to every person who has purchased and read Caterina's Adventure. I don't know how I can ever repay you!

-M.P.

Made in the USA
San Bernardino, CA
06 April 2014